Chapter 1: *Broad Daylig...*

Pamela stood on the edge of the sidewalk, watching the yellow police tape sway in the hot Austin breeze. She clutched the handle of her tote bag so tightly her knuckles turned white. The bag contained the lesson plans for her senior literature class—plans she wouldn't need today. Today was the day she buried her son.

Derrick Sinclair was only 29 years old, a bright young man with a career in engineering ahead of him. He'd been shot three times outside a coffee shop on Congress Avenue. Witnesses said it happened in broad daylight. They said the shooter didn't even bother to run.

Pamela had heard the suspect's name whispered among reporters: Clayton Reid. Wealthy, privileged, untouchable. She knew the type well—entitled young men whose families had deep pockets and even deeper connections. Men who never paid for their sins.

She held herself together at the funeral, accepting the murmured condolences of colleagues and neighbors. But as the sun set and the mourners drifted away, she made a silent vow. If justice wouldn't come for Derrick, she would deliver it herself.

Chapter 2: *The Double Life Begins*

Pamela adjusted her pearl earrings and smoothed the hem of her navy dress as she prepared for the day. She had mastered the art of appearing composed, even as rage churned beneath the surface. At Austin Central High

School, she was adored—a compassionate teacher who always had time for her students. But once the final bell rang, she became someone else entirely.

That evening, she sat in her car outside Clayton Reid's mansion, studying the movements of the security guards. Her heart pounded as she rehearsed her plan. She wasn't impulsive; she had spent weeks gathering details, mapping every escape route.

The seduction came easily. Clayton, cocky and oblivious, didn't recognize the danger in the alluring older woman who invited him to her car. A drink laced with poison was all it took. As she drove away, Pamela felt a rush of satisfaction. It was only the beginning.

Chapter 3: *The First Ripple*

The city buzzed with news of Clayton Reid's death. The media speculated about everything from rivalries to botched robberies, but no one suspected Pamela Sinclair. She listened to the radio on her way to work, barely suppressing a smirk.

Pamela's colleagues noticed her new energy. "You're glowing, Pam," said Diane, the head of the English department. Pamela shrugged it off with a practiced laugh. If only they knew.

But Pamela wasn't careless. She spent her nights researching her next target—a pharmaceutical CEO accused of murdering his wife. Her criteria were simple: the crime had to be heinous, the suspect wealthy, and the justice system ineffective.

Chapter 4: *The Spider's Web*

Detective Marcus Vega leaned over the evidence board in his office, frowning at the growing list of high-profile deaths. He didn't believe in coincidences. Each victim was out on bond for murder. Each had powerful attorneys and airtight alibis.

"This isn't random," he said to his partner, Elena Cruz. "Someone's sending a message."

Pamela had no idea her activities had caught the attention of law enforcement. She was already planning her next move—a senator's son with a history of violent assaults. But cracks in her façade began to appear. A student caught her crying in the faculty lounge. A neighbor mentioned hearing strange noises late at night.

Chapter 5: *A Second Taste of Justice*

Pamela parked her car two blocks away from Senator Clayton's estate, her pulse steady despite the storm raging inside her mind. It was her second target in less than three weeks, and she had planned every detail meticulously. This wasn't just about revenge anymore; it was a mission—a crusade against the wealthy elite who thought they were untouchable.

The senator's son, Bryce Clayton, was infamous in Austin's tabloids. At 26, he had been charged with vehicular manslaughter while drunk driving. His victim? A single mother of three. Bryce had been released on bond the same day. Pamela knew his habits—he frequented a private club downtown and always drank too much before driving home.

Tonight, she was ready. Dressed in an elegant black dress that hugged her curves, she blended seamlessly into the club's elite clientele. Bryce spotted her immediately, his lecherous gaze locking on to her as if she were a prize.

She played the part of the willing seductress, laughing at his crude jokes and allowing him to lead her to his car. Once inside, she slipped a syringe from her clutch and plunged it into his neck. Bryce's body went limp. Pamela drove his car to an abandoned warehouse and set the scene to look like a drug deal gone wrong.

The next morning, the headlines exploded: "Senator's Son Found Dead in Apparent Homicide." Pamela sipped her coffee, satisfied.

Chapter 6: *Detective Vega's Suspicions*

Detective Marcus Vega stared at the crime scene photos spread across his desk. Something about the murders nagged at him. The victims weren't random. Each was wealthy, connected, and out on bond for murder charges.

He reviewed Bryce Clayton's autopsy report. Poison. A pattern was forming, but Vega needed more. He assigned his team to dig into the victims' backgrounds, hoping to find a connection.

Meanwhile, Vega's personal life began to suffer. His late nights at the precinct and obsession with the case strained his relationship with his fiancée, who accused him of being more married to his work than to her. Vega brushed off her complaints; he couldn't let this killer slip through his fingers.

Chapter 7: *A Close Call*

Pamela was confident, but not careless. She changed her routines, avoided the same routes, and kept her social life minimal. But one evening, as she exited a diner where she'd been tailing her next target, she noticed a man in a dark sedan watching her.

Her breath caught, but she forced herself to remain calm. Was it Vega? Or perhaps an investigator hired by one of the victims' families? She couldn't afford to find out.

Pamela ditched her car that night, taking a cab back to her modest suburban home. She spent the night reviewing her plans, searching for any mistakes she might have made. Her survival depended on perfection.

Chapter 8: *The School Rumors*

At school, Pamela maintained her warm, approachable demeanor, but the strain of her double life was starting to show. Her students noticed her sudden absences, and whispers began to circulate among the faculty.

"Do you think something's wrong with Mrs. Sinclair?" a student asked her classmate after Pamela abruptly left mid-lecture.

"Maybe she's still grieving her son," the classmate replied.

Pamela overheard the conversation and forced herself to smile. She couldn't let anyone suspect that her grief had transformed into something darker.

Chapter 9: *The Trap is Set*

Detective Vega decided to set a trap. He leaked information about a fabricated murder suspect out on bond, hoping to lure the killer into action.

Pamela saw the news report about the new suspect and felt her blood boil. Another murderer walking free? She couldn't let it slide. She began her research, unaware that the police were monitoring her movements more closely than ever.

Chapter 10: *A Night of Reckoning*

Pamela followed the fake suspect to a nightclub, her instincts screaming that something wasn't right. But her rage overpowered her caution. She lured him into an alley, ready to strike.

As she prepared to inject him, headlights flooded the alley. Vega and his team emerged, guns drawn. Pamela froze, her mind racing. She couldn't let them take her.

"Drop the syringe!" Vega commanded.

Pamela feigned surrender, then threw the syringe at Vega's face and bolted. Shots rang out, but she disappeared into the night.

Chapter 11: *The Escape*

Pamela sprinted down the narrow alley, her heart pounding as the shouts of officers echoed behind her. The alley ended in a high chain-link fence. With no time to think, she scrambled up, the wire cutting into her palms as she pulled herself over.

She landed hard on the other side, pain shooting up her leg, but she didn't stop. She darted into a nearby park, disappearing into the shadows of the trees. When the coast was clear, she pulled her phone from her pocket and activated a preprogrammed app. Within seconds, all her devices remotely wiped themselves clean.

Her double life was unraveling, but she wasn't done yet.

Chapter 12: *Undercover*

Pamela couldn't risk going home. Instead, she drove to an old cabin she'd rented months ago under a false name. It was secluded, surrounded by dense woods—a perfect hideout.

She spent the next few days monitoring the news. Detective Vega's name was all over the headlines. The media called her "The Bond Killer," and Vega was painted as the hero closing in on her.

Pamela couldn't afford to be careless anymore. She dyed her hair a soft chestnut brown, swapped her elegant dresses for casual jeans and hoodies, and began scouting her next move.

Chapter 13: *Vega's Growing Obsession*

Detective Vega was furious. His trap had nearly worked, but "The Bond Killer" had outsmarted him. He was sure of one thing: the killer wasn't a typical criminal. They were calculating, intelligent, and disciplined.

"What kind of person can live a double life like this?" Vega muttered as he pored over profiles of possible suspects.

"Maybe they're not who we think they are," Elena Cruz, his partner, said. "Someone ordinary. Invisible."

Her words struck a chord. Vega ordered his team to dig deeper into the victims' connections, searching for anyone with a personal vendetta.

Chapter 14: *The Reunion*

Pamela's next target was James Lawson, a corrupt real estate mogul who had been acquitted of killing a whistleblower. His arrogance was legendary, and Pamela knew he'd be easy to bait.

She posed as a journalist and arranged an interview with him under a fake name. Lawson, ever the narcissist, welcomed her into his penthouse.

As they sipped wine, Pamela felt a pang of regret. This was the life she could've had—wealth, influence, power—if her son hadn't been stolen from her. But the thought only fueled her resolve.

Lawson didn't notice the needle until it was too late.

Chapter 15: *The Pattern Emerges*

Lawson's death reignited public panic. Vega recognized the method immediately. "She's escalating," he told Cruz. "The kills are getting bolder."

Meanwhile, Pamela returned to her classroom, her students none the wiser. But cracks in her façade were forming. A parent-teacher conference ended abruptly when a parent mentioned the growing number of murders in Austin. Pamela's hands trembled as she dismissed the topic.

She couldn't hide forever, but she couldn't stop either.

Chapter 16: *Vega Closes In*

Vega's team finally found a pattern. All the victims were tied to high-profile cases in Austin, and most had been represented by the same defense attorney.

It was Cruz who made the breakthrough. "Look at this," she said, pointing to a list of teachers who had written letters to the judge in one of the cases.

Vega's blood ran cold when he saw Pamela Sinclair's name.

Chapter 17: *The Confrontation*

Vega decided to confront Pamela directly. He visited her classroom under the pretense of giving a guest lecture on criminal justice. Pamela's heart raced as Vega entered the room, his piercing gaze locking on her.

"Thank you for having me, Mrs. Sinclair," he said, his voice calm but probing. "I've heard you're an incredible teacher."

Pamela forced a smile, but the tension was palpable. She couldn't let him rattle her. "My students are lucky to have professionals like you share their knowledge," she replied, her voice steady.

But Vega wasn't fooled.

Chapter 18: *A Fatal Mistake*

Pamela decided she had to eliminate Vega. He was too close, and she couldn't risk him connecting her to the murders.

She followed him one evening after he left the precinct, but Vega was prepared. He'd anticipated her move and had backup waiting.

Pamela barely escaped, but now she knew the game had changed. She was no longer the hunter—she was the prey.

Chapter 19: *The Confession*

Cornered and desperate, Pamela decided to make one last move. She recorded a video confession, detailing her motives and the failures of the justice system.

"Maybe they'll call me a monster," she said into the camera. "But someone had to do something."

She left the video on a flash drive in an anonymous envelope addressed to Vega.

Chapter 20: *The Final Stand*

Will she escape once again, or will Vega finally bring her to justice?

Chapter 21: *The Breaking Point*

Pamela felt the noose tightening. Vega's relentless pursuit was unlike anything she'd anticipated. The media's obsession with "The Bond Killer" had turned her once-hidden mission into a public spectacle.

She decided to make her final move—one that would either secure her freedom or destroy everything. Vega was the key. If she eliminated him, the investigation would collapse.

Pamela spent days studying Vega's routine, watching his every move. The detective, in turn, had grown more cautious, anticipating her strike. What neither of them realized was how their battle had become deeply personal.

Chapter 22: *The Ambush*

Under the cover of darkness, Pamela infiltrated Vega's home. It was a calculated risk, but desperation fueled her every step. Inside, she found him seated at his desk, reviewing a case file.

"I figured you'd come," Vega said without looking up.

Pamela froze, her pistol aimed at him. "Then why are you still here?"

Vega turned to face her, his expression calm but intense. "Because I need answers. Why, Pamela? Why throw your life away for this?"

"You wouldn't understand," she said, her voice cold. "Justice isn't something people like you give. It's something people like me take."

Before she could fire, Vega's phone buzzed. Pamela's eyes flicked to it for a split second—just long enough for Vega to lunge.

They fought viciously, their movements a mix of raw emotion and survival instinct. Pamela managed to knock

Vega unconscious, but the sound of sirens approaching told her she had little time to escape.

Chapter 23: *The Disappearance*

Pamela fled the scene, leaving Vega alive but shaken. She knew the walls were closing in. Every safe house, every false identity, was now compromised.

But Pamela had one final trick up her sleeve: a passport and a plane ticket to Costa Rica, stored in a safety deposit box she'd opened years ago.

She made her way to the airport, blending in with the late-night travelers. Vega, recovering from their confrontation, realized too late what her plan was. By the time he alerted authorities, Pamela was already in the air.

Chapter 24: *A New Beginning*

In a small, secluded village in Costa Rica, Pamela sat on the porch of a modest bungalow, staring out at the ocean. She wasn't sure if she felt relief or emptiness.

She had left behind her life as a teacher, her son's memory haunting her every step. But she wasn't done. Not yet. The world was full of people like the ones she'd hunted in Austin, and Pamela knew her mission wasn't over.

Chapter 25: *Vega's Resolve*

Detective Vega stood in his office, staring at the map of Austin's murders. He had failed to catch her, but he wasn't giving up.

"She'll slip up eventually," Cruz said, handing him a cup of coffee.

"Maybe," Vega replied. "But she's not just a killer. She's a symbol. And symbols have a way of inspiring others."

As he turned off his desk lamp, Vega made a silent vow: the next time he and Pamela crossed paths, there would be no escape.

Epilogue: *The Message*

Weeks later, Vega received a package at the precinct. Inside was a handwritten note and a photo of a beach.

The note read:

"You'll never find me, but I'll be watching. Until next time."

It was signed with a simple "P."